DANCING WITH
Stories fro

D0614248

These stories come from different countries in Africa. First, there is a passenger on a plane, flying home to South Africa, talking to the stranger sitting next to him, a beautiful young Greek girl. Next, in Tanzania, Yasmin is very uncomfortable when a visiting professor asks her to dance with him. What *will* her mother say? In Uganda, strangers are brought together by the accidents of war – Atita, looking for a lost friend, and Okema, a young boy hiding from the rebels that steal children from the villages. And in the busy city of Johannesburg Caleb finds a new worry to add to the many worries in his life. But then he meets a stranger in a bar, who has the answer to it all . . .

BOOKWORMS WORLD STORIES

English has become an international language, and is used on every continent, in many varieties, for all kinds of purposes. *Bookworms World Stories* are the latest addition to the Oxford Bookworms Library. Their aim is to bring the best of the world's stories to the English language learner, and to celebrate the use of English for storytelling all around the world.

Jennifer Bassett
Series Editor

OXFORD BOOKWORMS LIBRARY
World Stories

Dancing with Strangers
Stories from Africa

Stage 3 (1000 headwords)

Series Editor: Jennifer Bassett
Founder Editor: Tricia Hedge
Activities Editors: Jennifer Bassett and Christine Lindop

NOTES ON THE ILLUSTRATORS

KWAME NYONG'O (illustrations on pages 4, 9, 13) was born in Chicago, USA, and now lives in Nairobi in Kenya. He has been a freelance artist for many years, working in book illustration, animation, and character design. He is also a teacher and runs art workshops. These are his first illustrations for a book for English language learners.

PETERSON KAMWATHI (illustrations on pages 17, 22) was born in 1980 in Nairobi, Kenya, and started painting after high school. He has had three solo art exhibitions, and taken part in many group exhibitions. These are his first book illustrations.

JOSEPH NTENSIBE (illustrations on pages 29, 34, 39) was born in 1951 in Uganda, East Africa. A freelance artist for many years, he works in oils, ink, pencil and charcoal, and watercolours, and his artworks have been shown in galleries in Kenya and the USA. These are his first book illustrations.

MESHACK ASARE (illustrations on pages 43, 49, 54) was born in 1945 in Ghana. He studied Art, and later Social Anthropology, and was a teacher for many years. He is now a very well-known writer and illustrator of children's books, and travels widely through Africa looking for different African cultures to represent in his stories. His books have won numerous awards, including Noma and UNESCO awards, and have been published in many countries.

RETOLD BY CLARE WEST

Dancing with Strangers

Stories from Africa

OXFORD UNIVERSITY PRESS

OXFORD
UNIVERSITY PRESS

Great Clarendon Street, Oxford OX2 6DP

Oxford University Press is a department of the University of Oxford.
It furthers the University's objective of excellence in research, scholarship,
and education by publishing worldwide in

Oxford New York

Auckland Cape Town Dar es Salaam Hong Kong Karachi
Kuala Lumpur Madrid Melbourne Mexico City Nairobi
New Delhi Shanghai Taipei Toronto

With offices in

Argentina Austria Brazil Chile Czech Republic France Greece
Guatemala Hungary Italy Japan Poland Portugal Singapore
South Korea Switzerland Thailand Turkey Ukraine Vietnam

OXFORD and OXFORD ENGLISH are registered trade marks of
Oxford University Press in the UK and in certain other countries

ISBN: 978 0 19 479197 7

A complete recording of this Bookworms edition of *Dancing with Strangers:
Stories from Africa* is available on audio CD ISBN 978 0 19 479161 8

Printed in Hong Kong

ACKNOWLEDGEMENTS
The publishers are grateful to the following for permission to adapt and simplify copyright texts:
to the author Jackee Budesta Batanda for *Remember Atita*, first published on
http://www.author-me.com/fict04; to Michael Cope and Raymond Cope for *Ekaterina*,
first published in *The Man who Doubted and Other Stories* by Jack Cope; to the author Mandla Langa
and to David Philip of New Africa Books for *A Gathering of Bald Men*, first published in *World
Literature Today*; to the author M. G. Vassanji and McClelland & Stewart Ltd for *Breaking Loose*, from
Uhuru Street (McClelland & Stewart Ltd, 1992/Heinemann International Literature and textbooks,
1991). Copyright © 1992 M. G. Vassanji. With permission of the author.

Cover image shows a detail from *Utex Africa Oye (Long Live Utex Africa)* by Moké (Monsengwo
Kejwamfi), 1989, Oil on canvas, 113 x 180 cm, © Moké, by kind permission of the C.A.A.C.,
The Pigozzi Collection, Geneva

Word count (main text): 11,990 words

For more information on the Oxford Bookworms Library,
visit www.oup.com/elt/bookworms

CONTENTS

NOTE ON THE LANGUAGE

There are many varieties of English spoken in the world, used by people who speak many other languages as well. In these stories set in Africa there are a few words from African languages such as Swahili and Acholi. All these words are either explained in the stories or in the glossary on page 57.

Ekaterina

JACK COPE

◻◻◻

A story from South Africa, retold by Clare West

In some countries, young people marry a person chosen for them by their parents. Sometimes these arranged marriages work very well; and sometimes they don't.

It becomes more difficult when there are questions of money, or of distance. Perhaps the man's family is rich, and the girl's family is poor. Perhaps the two families live in different parts of the world. From Greece to South Africa, for example, is a long, long way . . .

*C*oming into Athens. The man in the next seat put away some papers, looking bored.

'Air travel has changed our idea of place, time, country,' I said to him. 'In fact, there aren't countries any more, in the way we used to think of them. Nowhere is more than twenty-four hours away. Soon, the idea of having different countries will just disappear.'

He laughed.

'What's so strange about that?' I said. 'And yet where I came from, there are still people who measure distance by days. "He lives two days' walk away," they say.'

'Are we talking about life in this century?' he said.

The man was an American, and I had to explain what

things were like in parts of Africa. I'd lived in some of its wilder places during my fifty years.

'And now we can travel at the speed of sound,' I went on, 'but we're like children. We don't know what to do when we get there.'

He thought I was a little crazy. 'If you come from South Africa, you should be black and speak Zulu,' he said.

'I do speak Zulu,' was my answer.

He left the plane at Athens, and I was not sorry to see him go. Johannesburg was another twelve hours away.

I had not travelled through Athens before, so I ran down the steps from the plane to put my foot for the first time on Greek soil. I thought back two and a half thousand years, to the time of ancient Greece. Did those great writers, Euripides and Aristophanes, once walk where I walked now? Did they see these same white and gold hills, breathe this same air?

It was late afternoon, and a soft summer light lay on those distant white hills. Over the smell of hot engine oil around the airport, I told myself I could smell the sweet clean air of ancient Greece. I was not looking at faceless passengers hurrying into a crowded airport, but could see girls with flowers in their hair, dancing to ancient music, for ancient gods. And away to the north of the airport Athens called to me, that city of light, the birthplace of the Western world, but I had no time to visit. I had to board my plane again.

At the entrance to the airport building, a few bright flowers grew in dry, dusty soil. A young man with bad teeth stopped to offer me picture postcards of Athens.

Then a bewildered little group of men and women came

into the airport building. The men, in poor best clothes, had big red hands. The women carried boxes and packets, and one of the men had a cheap suitcase. A young girl at their centre, wearing a yellow suit which looked uncomfortably new, stared around her at the strangeness of everything. She looked straight at me with the same bewilderment, smiled and turned away. Her face had a beauty that was centuries old – large dark eyes, a short straight nose, and a lovely mouth. There was a circle of white star-like flowers in her long black hair.

The light still touched the ring of hills as the sun went down. When the same sun rose again for me, it would be red and wintry over South Africa. Why not leave the plane here, and find a little house somewhere? Maybe there was a deeper, quieter peace in these ancient hills than in other places.

But they were calling my flight. I ran for the plane and was the last to board it. The next seat to mine, left empty by the American, was now taken by the young girl in the yellow suit. She stood up at once to welcome me, speaking in her own language, and gave me her hand. She moved with all the naturalness of a wild animal. There had been tears in her eyes.

Back in her seat, she was looking out of the window, trying to see the tiny figures far away across the runway. She waved a hand that no one would see. The plane's engines started up. I saw that a finger of the hand at the window carried the shining gold circle of a new wedding ring.

She cried in silence, as the plane took off and rose heavily into the sky. We could see the dark blue sea below, and far to the west, the path of the dying sun on the water.

*The young girl at the centre of the group stared around her
at the strangeness of everything.*

Flying was clearly a new experience for her. She said something quietly, shaking her head in wonder. The sadness left her, and a minute later she touched my arm and excitedly pointed out something. Athens was disappearing into the sea and the night; already we were rising through the clouds.

I decided to go back to reading my magazine. There was no way of making polite conversation, and it seemed useless to look at her just because she was very good to look at. But she seemed not to realize there was a language difficulty.

'Ekaterina,' she said, pointing to herself.

I told her my name – Neil Gordon. We shook hands again, and she was delighted that we could understand each other so easily. We continued our conversation using expressions and hand movements, and in answer to her questions, I explained that I was not an Englishman, a German, or an American. I was a South African, living in Johannesburg.

'Ah! Yoannisburg!' That was where she was going. She looked very pleased, and went on talking. There was a warm feeling between us – we seemed like close friends. Sometimes her face changed and she looked sad, as she turned the ring on her finger. Then suddenly she smiled and became cheerful again. I did not understand her words, but that did not matter. She was like a child talking to herself in the night, or a mother telling her thoughts to her baby.

The air hostess was passing, and I said to her, 'Do you understand Greek?'

'Not a word,' she replied, 'but one of the other passengers looks Greek, so I'll ask him.'

A minute later she was back. 'I'm sorry,' she said, 'he

isn't Greek, he's Italian. But he says he'd be very pleased to change seats with you and talk to the young lady.'

'Tell him,' I said, 'to stay in his own seat. I'm very happy where I am.'

The lights inside the plane had come on. The girl took off her jacket and, smiling, asked my opinion of the blouse that she was wearing. Unlike her factory-made suit, it was a beautiful thing. Clearly she had made it herself, and hours of careful work had gone into the patterns of flowers and leaves. I told her how lovely it was. She watched my expression carefully, her face blushing a little.

Her eyes became serious. She sat thinking for a moment, and then she decided. She took her passport from her bag, and put it into my hands. It was a passport of my own country, with Ekaterina's frightened little face looking out of the photograph. How did she come to have a South African passport? She had never left Greece.

But explaining this to me wasn't difficult. She had married a South African, married him that morning, in fact. And her husband? He was in Yoannisburg. She was going to meet him there. She had never seen him. The marriage had been by proxy. Her parents had arranged it. I began to understand the whole thing. The husband had paid for everything. He had paid for her. He had sent money for the plane ticket.

I asked the air hostess to bring a bottle of wine, to drink to Ekaterina's happiness. The Italian passenger came to see her. I told him Ekaterina had been married that morning, and invited him to join us in a drink. He tried Italian, Spanish, and German on her, but she only looked at him, surprised.

He drank to her happiness and kissed her hand, which was small and strong, a working girl's hand.

'She is too beautiful,' he said to me. 'Are you taking her to her husband?'

'Certainly not. In fact, I want her to run away with me, and there's a good chance she'll agree to it.'

'She is just a child.'

'I know how old she is, I've seen her passport. Do you still want to talk to her?'

He shook his head and went back to his seat. Ekaterina said something and smiled. She drank her wine slowly, and in a moment was lost in her own thoughts again. Her beauty was timeless, centuries old, untouchable. But the soft light in her eyes and the shine of her dark hair brought her into the present for me – here and now, sitting beside me, a warm, living, breathing girl.

She turned to me, looking serious. She put her hands together in front of her, to show that she was asking for my help with something very important. Then she calmly handed me a photograph. It was of a young man, about twenty-eight or thirty. He had thick dark hair; the face was generous in its way, strong if not handsome, and the eyes were pleasantly gentle. The photo had been cut out of a larger photo, but enough was left to show that behind the young man was a shining new car.

Who? It was her husband, of course, whom she had never seen. She told me his name: 'Savvas Athanassiades.' I hadn't looked up from the photograph, but I knew she was watching me carefully. Standing next to the car, Savvas looked unusually short. I had owned a car like that myself, many years ago. But why did Savvas want a photograph of himself in front of a thirty-year-old Chevrolet, shiny or not?

'A good man,' I said. 'Let's drink to Savvas Athanassiades.' I avoided her eyes, pouring more wine into our glasses. But her woman's instinct told her something was wrong; I could feel that she didn't believe me. Slowly and miserably she put away her photograph. Then she noticed her glass and lifted it. 'Yoannisburg,' she said.

'Athena,' I replied. She repeated it and added with a sad smile, 'Vari.' I did not know the town of Vari, but wherever it was, it was the place where she had left her dreams.

Dinner was the usual kind of tasteless meal that you get on planes. I showed Ekaterina how to hold her knife and fork, and she got through it by watching and copying. From time to time she looked happily at me, her face a little pink from the wine. To her, it was all new and strange and wonderful.

We came down at Khartoum and left the plane for an hour. Ekaterina kept close to me as we walked to the airport building through the hot, breathless African night. There were sleepy flies on the dirty tables in the restaurant. We drank a warm, sweet drink that tasted of soap. A man came through the restaurant, selling things. He showed Ekaterina a piece of cheap silk, and her eyes shone with delight. I offered to buy it for her. She thanked me, but no, it was impossible. Not because I was a stranger, no, that wasn't it. Perhaps because she couldn't give anything back. Then the man put a fan into her hand. It was worth almost nothing, and I paid

I could feel that Ekaterina didn't believe me. Her woman's instinct told her that something was wrong.

too much for it. But that was different – a fan was necessary in the heat.

The plane took off again, lifting up over sleeping Africa. For a short time the River Nile looked silver in the moonlight, until it was lost in the darkness. We went on climbing alone into the milky sky. The passengers started preparing themselves for sleep. Ekaterina turned towards the window, and I lay back in my seat, horribly uncomfortable.

About half an hour later I woke up. Like a newborn animal, Ekaterina had moved as close as possible to me. One arm was round my neck, and her face was half hidden in my shoulder. She smelt sweet and warm, like wild flowers or deep, newly turned soil. She was asleep, and in her dreams she had returned to Vari, to a street of quiet little houses, to a single room full of sisters and brothers, with animals to take care of, perhaps. Had she ever slept alone? Who was I in her sleep, who was held in her poor arms? A little brother who was always crying, a sister restless with hunger? How could her family have sold this lovely child to an unknown husband? Perhaps he was an honest man who had earned his place in South Africa. And now he was looking back into the past, to take a wife of his own country, of the blood of Greece. I only hoped he was good enough for her. I tried to tell myself, 'She's nothing to me. What does it matter who she marries?' But it wasn't easy to say that, when she was actually asleep and warm and living against my body.

I slept a little, and when I woke up, Ekaterina had not moved. But she was now awake, and her large eyes were fixed darkly on me. How long had she stared at me like that?

'Hello, Ekaterina,' I said.

'Ello.' She closed her eyes, preparing for sleep again.

'Ekaterina, I'm talking to you.'

A little movement of her head showed that she was awake.

'Listen, it may be a good thing that you don't understand. Listen, Ekaterina, you shouldn't be here. Go back, take the first chance to go back. This marriage may work, but it may not. It's all wrong. You're not a thing for a man to buy, you're not a prisoner. It's so important to be free. Go back and learn to be free. They've taken the past from you and you're throwing away the future. Ekaterina, it's always better to die fighting – you must know that.'

I was talking almost to myself. She could not understand a word, but something in my voice frightened her. She began to cry. The great plane went on into the silken blackness. Under us lay Africa, sleeping in the long night wind.

She cried quietly, but not for long. I think she was used to having sadness in her life. She took my hand and kissed it before I could stop her – a little show of grateful feeling which I found very moving. Then she dried her eyes, and talked brightly for a few minutes like a playful child. Soon she fell asleep, and her arms reached out again towards me, in that instinctively loving way of hers.

We came in over South Africa before daylight. People began to wake up. I went to have a wash, and when I got back, I found Ekaterina very unhappy. She and the air hostess were looking everywhere for something. The Italian was there too, down on his hands and knees to help with the search.

'What are you looking for?' I asked him.

He stood up, looking angrily at me. 'The girl's miserable. What have you done to her?'

'You haven't slept well, I suppose?'

'Slept! I never sleep well on a plane.'

'You should find another way of travelling.'

He went crossly back to his seat. Ekaterina asked me to help, but I had no idea what was missing. Had it disappeared at Khartoum?

'Khartoum!' She threw up her hands in the air. Yes, perhaps the people at Khartoum had robbed her. Then suddenly a passenger a few seats away held up a packet of newspapers. Ah, that was it – yesterday's Greek papers, for the good Savvas to read. The evening news from Athena arriving in Yoannisburg the next morning. Lucky man.

I helped Ekaterina off the plane with her bags and packets. The air was cold, and she looked around her, frightened. I lost her in the crowd at the passport desks, and did not see her again until we were in the main hall of the airport building. There she was in a group of four or five people. Her head was low and her face was hidden in her hands. I could not see which was Savvas; there was nobody who looked like the man in her photograph.

She lifted her head and stared around. Then she saw me and came running down the hall. She put her head, like a child, on my shoulder, crying miserably. The little group of strangers watched from a distance. Now I saw that Savvas, the new husband himself, was there. It was certainly the man from the photograph, but he was bald and old, and very short and fat. I had half expected it.

Ekaterina put her head on my shoulder, crying miserably.
The little group of strangers watched from a distance.

'Ekaterina, I'll help you get back if you wish, to Athena, to Vari . . .'

I gave her my business card, with my address and phone number, and she stared at it through tearful eyes. She took my hand and held it for a moment. Then she dried her eyes and walked slowly back to the waiting group, her head held high.

My son and his wife, Loraine, found me standing there. I had not moved, and was staring after Ekaterina.

'Who's that beautiful little thing?' Loraine asked.

'Ekaterina.'

'Is it a love story?'

'I don't know. I think it's more like an unhappy ending.'

They were amused, and laughed about it while we had breakfast in the airport's large, cheerful restaurant.

'It's possible you've got it all wrong,' said Loraine. 'Remember, you couldn't understand what she was saying.'

'My instinct tells me I'm right.'

'Your instinct! Only a woman can be sure of her instinct.'

Why didn't I speak to Savvas Athanassiades at the airport? I do not know where to find him. His name is not in the phone book. I have waited to hear from Ekaterina, but nothing, not a word. Where is she? I remember how she walked calmly away, with her head up. Her dark shining hair, the yellow of her suit . . . Choosing to go, walking freely into a darkened future . . . But after all, perhaps Loraine is right.

I have heard nothing, and it is now four days.

Breaking Loose

M. G. VASSANJI

⸙ ⸙ ⸙

A story from Tanzania, retold by Clare West

Where do we come from, where do we belong, where is home? Easy questions, but the answers are not always so simple. Family, culture, history – all these things connect in different and mysterious ways.

An Asian girl and an African man meet at a university dance in an African country. It is the girl's home town, and the man is a visitor from another country. Who is the foreigner here . . . and does it matter?

band called Iblis was playing on the stage. The singer and guitarist was a young Asian with long hair, now singing another popular foreign song. Close to the stage danced a group of fashionable, brightly dressed girls. Their wild way of dancing seemed to say that they were the girlfriends of the four young men in the band.

Yasmin was at the far end of the dance floor with her girlfriends. She and two of the girls were standing, because there weren't enough chairs. Sometimes she looked round at the dancers and the band, hoping to see an empty chair that she could bring over. The band was loud, the room was hot and airless, and everyone was sweating. A well-dressed black man in a grey suit appeared out of the crowd of dancers. He came up to her and asked her to dance. She went.

Of all the girls here, why me? I don't want to dance. I can't dance, she thought. From the centre of the dance floor she looked back sadly at her friends, who were talking and laughing in the distance.

'I'm sorry,' he smiled. 'I took you away from your friends.'

'It's okay . . . only for a few minutes—' she began, and blushed, realizing that was not a polite answer. *After all, I should be pleased*, she thought. *He's a professor.*

It was a dance that did not need any closeness or touching – and she was grateful for that.

'Daniel Akoto. That's my name.'

'I know . . . I'm Yasmin Rajan.'

It's all so unnecessary, she thought. *I'm not the type. Why didn't he dance with one of those girls near the stage?*

She looked at him. He danced much better than she did.

She was shorter than him. Her long hair was brushed straight back from her face, and she wore a simple dress. This was the middle of her second year at the university.

'Good music,' he said.

'Yes, isn't it? I know the singer—'

'But too Western, don't you think?'

'I don't know . . .'

She felt uncomfortable with the conversation. There was the little worry too – why had he chosen her, and would he want to see her again? He was looking at her and still talking.

'. . . you're too westernized, you Asians. You like Western ways, European ways, even more than we Africans do.'

Daniel Akoto was looking at her and still talking.
'. . . you're too westernized, you Asians.'

She didn't know what to reply, and felt very embarrassed.

He went on, shaking his head, 'Just listen to that song! Rolling Stones. What do you call Indian in that? Or am I missing something?'

Oh, why doesn't he stop? she thought. 'What do you mean, we're westernized?' she said angrily. 'Of course we have our own culture. We have centuries-old customs . . .'

She had stopped dancing and there were tears in her eyes. She felt under attack in the middle of the two hundred people dancing around her. She could feel their eyes burning into her, seeing her embarrassment.

She left Akoto in the middle of the dance floor and, with her back straight and her head high, returned to her friends.

▦ ▦ ▦

The next day she waited for her punishment. A call to the university's head office, a black mark for her rudeness to a professor who was a visitor from another African country.

During lunch in the university restaurant with her friends, she saw him standing at the door, looking around the room. She took a deep breath and waited. His eyes found her and he hurried forward between the tables, laughing and calling out greetings to people as he passed. When he arrived at her table, he found an empty chair, sat down and looked at her.

'About last night . . .' he began. The other girls picked up their plates and left.

She laughed. 'You pushed them out,' she said. 'They'll hate you for that.' She wondered where she had found the confidence to speak like that to him. He was in a red shirt – expensive, she thought. He looked handsome – and harmless.

'But not for long, I hope,' he began. His smile grew wider as he looked at her. 'I've come to apologize. I asked you for a dance and then I bored you with all those ideas of mine.'

'It's okay. It's my fault too. You see . . .'

'I know, I know. An innocent Indian girl having to dance with a man! But tell me – don't you expect men to ask you to dance when you're in a dance hall with music playing?'

She smiled, a little embarrassed. 'Having girlfriends with you usually means that strangers don't come and ask . . .'

'Oh dear! I'm a foreigner, so I didn't know that! You came to have a good time with your friends but you couldn't, because of me. I'm really sorry. Look, let me show you how sorry I am. I'll take you for a drink. How about that?'

'But I don't drink . . . alcohol, I mean.'

'Don't worry. We'll find something for you.'

It was wrong of him to ask her, of course, but she found she had accepted his invitation without any worries.

When they met, as arranged, later that afternoon, he said, 'I'll take you to The Matumbi.' The Matumbi was a tea shop under a tree, half a mile from the university. It had a roof but no walls. She went in slowly, feeling a little shy. But Akoto was well known there, and the owner pulled up two chairs at a table for them.

'Are you hungry?' Akoto asked.

'No. I'll just have tea . . . perhaps a small cake . . .'

'Right! Two teas, one cake and one sikisti!' he called out.

'What's a sikisti?' she asked.

'It's a hot egg sandwich. It's called sikisti because it costs sixty cents!'

She laughed.

'It's true, believe me!'

Akoto was a professor of sociology, from Ghana.

'What are you studying?' he asked her, after their tea.

'Literature.'

'Do you read any African writers?'

'Yes. Soyinka . . . Achebe . . .'

'*Things fall apart . . .*' he said.

'*The centre cannot hold.*' She finished the words for him.

He laughed. 'What about Ngugi? Palangyo? Omari?'

She shook her head. She hadn't heard of them.

'New, local writers. You should read Nuru Omari. *Wait for Me*, that's her first book. I could lend it to you if you want.'

'It's okay. I'll borrow it from the library.'

He looked very surprised. 'But it'll take a long time for the library to get it.'

'I'll wait . . . I don't have much time right now.'

'All right.' He was annoyed.

At last, when he saw that she was a little restless, he said, 'Well, now that I've apologized, I hope . . . Well, perhaps we can go.'

I am studying literature and I have no time to read the most recent books, she thought. She felt ashamed.

▨ ▨ ▨

When she saw him again several days later, he did not appear to notice her.

He knows I'm not interested, she thought. *So why did I go to the tea shop with him? . . . Because he's so different, so confident, so intelligent . . . He's a real gentleman! Ah, that's*

it! He said we Asians are westernized, but what about him?
He's a perfect English gentleman himself! I'll tell him that!

'Dear Professor Akoto,' she wrote, 'I wanted to tell you something. You called us Asians westernized. Well, have you looked at yourself recently? Your language, your clothes – a suit even in hot weather – you are just like an English gentleman yourself! Yours sincerely, Yasmin Rajan. P.S. Could I borrow Omari's *Wait for Me* from you after all? Thanks.' She put the note under his office door.

The next day he came to find her at lunchtime again.

'You're quite right,' he said. 'Although I'm not sure I completely agree . . . But let's not argue. Let me show you my library. You can borrow any book you like.'

He took her to his house, and when he opened the door of his sitting room, her eyes opened wide in surprise. Three of the walls were covered with books. She had never before seen so many books which belonged to one person.

'You've read all these books?' she asked.

'Well . . . I wouldn't . . .'

'Lucky you. You must know so much!'

'Oh, not really.'

'Do you also write?'

'Yes. But none of my writing is published yet.'

He had ideas about African literature. 'Today's writers are going back to their beginnings, digging deep. And that's what I'm trying to do – dig. So you can understand why I worry about what's real and what isn't.'

They went to The Matumbi that evening. She had her first sikisti, and talked about her family.

*At The Matumbi that evening, Yasmin had her first sikisti,
and talked about her family.*

'My father had a pawnshop, but pawnshops are no longer allowed, so now he has a shop which makes men's clothes. Tell me, do you think pawnshops are a bad thing?'

'Well, I think they're bad for poor people. They have to pay an awful lot to get their things back.'

'But where *can* poor people borrow money from? Not the banks! And you should see the kind of things they bring to the pawnshop. Old watches, broken bicycles, sometimes clothes. We have three old gramophones that we can't sell.'

'Is that right? Can I look at them? Perhaps I'll buy one. I like unfashionable old things.'

So one afternoon Yasmin took him to her father's shop to show him the old gramophones. He entered the shop alone, while Yasmin went round to the back of the building, where the family lived. Her father came to meet Akoto.

'Come in, Bwana. What can I get for you?'

'I came with Yasmin,' Akoto explained in his bad Swahili. 'For a gramophone . . .'

'Ah, yes! The professor! Sit, Bwana, sit.'

While Yasmin's father showed Akoto the gramophones, Yasmin was inside the house, talking to her mother.

'How can you bring him here like this?' said her mother angrily. 'What will the neighbours think? I'm so ashamed!'

'But Mummy, he is a professor!'

'I don't care if he's a professor's father!'

By the time Akoto had left the shop, with his gramophone, Yasmin's mother was wild with anger. 'You do *not* have friendships with men – not with men who we don't know.'

'The world is not ready for it,' said Yasmin's father quietly.

'You stay out of it!' his wife screamed. 'This is between Yasmin and me!'

Yasmin knew her father would discuss things sensibly, but her mother never stopped warning her, and punishing her, and expecting the worst, just because she was a girl. Yasmin's three brothers did not have this problem.

'What do you know of him? With an Asian man, even if he's very bad, you know what to expect. But with *him*?' Her mother went on shouting and screaming like this for hours.

By the end of the day Yasmin felt half dead with tiredness.

It was more than a week before she and Akoto met again.

'Where do you eat lunch these days?' he said, smiling. 'You're the perfect salesman. You sell me an old gramophone and disappear. Are you afraid I'll return it?'

She said something polite, and walked quickly away. Later she returned the books that she had borrowed from him, and refused an invitation to The Matumbi. She did not go to the end-of-year dance, but her friends told her what happened there. Professor Akoto sat alone at a table for a while, and drank quite a lot. He got into a fight with Mr Sharp of the Boys' School. Then he left.

India was not just the past, or the close circle of family, neighbours, and friends. India was a place, a culture, one of the great nations of the world. And during the holidays Yasmin discovered India. She read endlessly, and asked her father about it. Here in Africa she was an Asian, an Indian.

But up to now she had known almost nothing about India. At first, her search for her own past seemed to put a distance between her and Akoto, the African. But this was what he had talked about – digging deep, finding what was real. So in a strange way her search also brought her closer to him.

The world seemed a smaller place when she went back to university. Smaller but exciting; full of people doing their best, fighting, loving, staying alive. And she was one of those people. People who were locked into their own histories and customs were like prisoners, she thought. But sometimes the old patterns were broken, and things changed – lives changed, the world changed. She was part of that change, she decided.

A month later Yasmin's father was lifting boxes in his shop when he felt a pain in his heart. The doctor was called, but arrived late, and by then Yasmin's father was dead.

Daniel Akoto came to the funeral. He sat on the ground among the men, sweating and uncomfortable, trying to sit with his legs crossed. A black face in a sea of patient brown Asian faces. Someone saw how uncomfortable he was and put out a chair for him by the wall. From there Akoto could see clearly across the room.

Mrs Rajan sat beside the dead man, crying. When she looked up, she saw Akoto through her tears, and lost control.

'You!' she screamed. 'What are you doing here? What kind of man are you, who comes to take away my daughter, even in my sadness? Who asked you to come? Go away!'

People turned to stare. Akoto gave an apologetic smile.

'Go!' said the woman wildly, pointing a finger at the door.

No one else said a word. Akoto stood up, bent his head respectfully towards the dead man and left the room.

A week later Yasmin knocked at his door late in the evening and found him in.

'Come in,' he said, putting away his pipe.

'I've come to apologize for what happened at the funeral.'

'It's all right. People aren't at their best at a funeral . . . but perhaps they're more honest.' He watched her face carefully.

'You must think we're awful. You're a professor – you know so much – you're a great man . . .'

'No, I don't think you're awful. And don't call me a great man!'

She began to laugh, a little wildly. They both laughed.

'And you, I respect you.' He spoke calmly. 'You are brave. You left that crowd of girls that day at the dance, and since then you've done it again and again. It's brave, what you've done. Trying to break away from family, friends, the old customs, the old ways . . . trying to find your own path in life . . . Even coming here like this. I realize that and I like you.'

'Well, I like you too!' she said, too quickly. There was a silence between them. 'You know, it's not going to be easy . . . with my father dead, this will be the most terrible news for my mother . . . it will kill her, it will . . .' Tears were running down her face.

'Now, now.' He went up to her, put her wet face on his shirt. 'We'll have to do the best we can, won't we?'

Remember Atita

JACKEE BUDESTA BATANDA

❖

A story from Uganda, retold by Clare West

When there is war in a country, it is easy to lose people. Mothers lose children, children lose parents, sisters lose brothers, friends lose friends . . .

Atita is in Gulu town, looking for her friends. All she has is an old photograph, taken eighteen years ago. At night she sleeps on shop verandas, with all the children from the villages, who are hiding from the rebels. It is a hopeless search, but Atita does not stop hoping . . .

We're five of the Ten Green Bottles in the nursery rhyme that we sang all those years ago in 1985. Five Green Bottles standing on the wall of life. Five bright smiling faces stare out of the old black and white photo. Our arms are round each other's shoulders, and we're looking towards the camera, our eyes shining. We don't notice the torn clothes that we're wearing. Our legs are covered with brown soil. We smile through our missing teeth.

❖

2003. The photo of my past lies in my hands, with the edges torn. It's brown with age. It doesn't shine in the light from the shop signpost above me. I pass the photo to Okema, who sits next to me with his legs crossed. There are a lot of us here, sitting on the floor of the shop veranda. A radio is playing loud music.

I'm trying to explain to Okema why I've travelled back to Gulu town to search for the girls in the photo. We sit on the veranda because it's safer to spend the night in the town. The LRA rebels don't come to Gulu town; they only attack the villages. We talk quietly because we don't want to wake the other children, who are sleeping. Okema and I are kept awake by the fear of the night. We talk to hold this fear back. In the distance we hear gunshots from time to time.

The faces in the photo are like strangers. I've been away too long. I'm not sure they'll recognize me when we meet. I begin to get an empty feeling inside me. Tears fill my eyes. Okema takes my hand and whispers,

'It's all right to cry.'

Our eyes meet. I smile. My finger trembles as I pick out the faces. Laker stands close to me in the photo. She and I were born on the same day. We were more like sisters than friends. We had such fun together! She was the leader of the group, and always had the craziest ideas. I wonder what she looks like now. Perhaps she's tall and beautiful.

'Why did you leave Gulu?' Okema asks.

I am not sure how to answer. We leave places because we need to start a new life. I left because my grandfather, *Won* Okech, died. I had lived in his house since my parents' death, and after his death there was no one to take care of me. Then my mother's cousin, *min* Komakech, appeared like a rain cloud and took me away to help with her children.

*Okema and I talk quietly because we don't want to wake
the other children, who are sleeping.*

'I don't know,' I lie. I quickly start talking about something else. 'How many children are left in your family?'

'I'm the last of them,' he says. 'That's why my mother makes sure I come to town every evening.'

'I'm the only one in my family too,' I say.

We are two lonely stars.

Sometimes I think this search is hopeless. So much has happened since I last saw my friends. Perhaps they have died or the rebels have taken them away. But I know I have to find Laker. I know she needs me. All I have is this old photo, which no one recognizes. I spend my days under the sun, moving from place to place, but I get no answers.

Okema is asleep. I'd like to sleep too, but I can't. Okema gives a frightened cry in his sleep. I know he has the same dream every night. In his dream the rebels attack his home and take him away from his mother. That's what happened to all his brothers and sisters. And as they take him away, he can hear his mother's screams. He always wakes up then, and finds me staring at him. I tell him that he's safe, and that the rebels are only a bad dream. I pull him to me, put my arms around him and start singing quietly,

Ten green bottles standing on the wall,

Ten green bottles standing on the wall,

If one green bottle should accidentally fall . . .

Soon he stops crying and goes to sleep again. I know he has slept on verandas in town for almost a year now, hiding from the rebels that attack the villages. When the sun rises, he'll run home to his mother, who'll send him off to school. He's reading for his school-leaving examinations.

'I shall become President and end the war,' he says when he's feeling hopeful.

'I want to see my mother smile again,' he says when he's feeling miserable.

I go on singing the nursery rhyme as I look at the photo. We are five of the ten green bottles on the wall. And if one green bottle should accidentally fall . . . Which of us fell first?

✸

Gulu Hospital. I'm shaking with excitement. Laker is here. Someone guides me through the hospital, past patients lying on the floor. There are flies everywhere. I pass a bed where a little girl lies, crying with pain. She has no legs. An older woman sits beside her and tries to keep off the flies.

'A landmine,' the guide whispers to me. I stare straight ahead and try to walk faster.

When we reach Laker's bed, I see that she's asleep. We stand silently and wait. The smiling child in the photo has become this poor, sick woman. A torn blue blanket covers her body. The sheet on the bed is brown with dirt. I have waited four weeks for this moment. I was hoping we would laugh and talk about old times together. I did not expect our meeting to be in a hospital.

I hold out my hand to touch her, but the guide stops me. 'She's still sleeping,' he says. I say nothing. I wait.

Suddenly Laker's eyes fly open. She stares at us, with no expression. I smile at her. She continues to stare at me. Her thin face frightens me. Her skin is oily and wet. The heat is awful. Surely the blanket is too hot for her? I move closer.

'Laker,' I whisper, holding her thin hand. I don't think she remembers me. 'It's me, Atita,' I say. '*Won* Okech's grand-daughter, Atita.' I'm close to her, but I can't reach her.

She opens her mouth. '*Otoo. Won* Okech *otoo.*'

She's right. *Won* Okech is dead. He died over ten years ago. No one could forget *Won* Okech. I remember once I told him about a game that we had played with some older boys. We called it playing 'mummy and daddy'. When *Won* Okech heard that, he was very angry and beat the five of us girls very hard with his stick. We couldn't walk or sit for a week. My friends told me to keep my big mouth shut in future.

'Yes. *Won* Okech is dead,' I reply.

I want to know what happened to the others, but Laker still doesn't seem to recognize me. The guide tells me it's time to leave. I want to stay, but he won't let me. I bend down and whisper into Laker's ear, 'Laker, please remember Atita.'

❁

That evening on the shop veranda, Okema asks, 'Did you and she talk together? Did she remember you?'

'No.'

'Don't worry, *I* remember you. Look, I kept a sleeping place for you on the veranda.'

'She said my *Won* Okech was dead.'

'So that means she remembers . . .'

'No,' I say coldly, 'she doesn't. I want her to remember *me*. I want her to remember Atita.'

'I'm sorry,' says Okema.

'Let's not talk about it.'

The other children are restless. Sometimes a figure passes by our veranda or a dog runs past. But most of the time the town square where we sit is empty. The townspeople are locked up in their homes.

I stare ahead. Laker doesn't remember me. Laker doesn't remember Atita. Perhaps I have changed too much. I am a stranger to her. I am not the same Atita who she played with years ago. Time and distance have made us different people. It's the price that we have to pay in the game called life.

I haven't found out why she's in Gulu Hospital. Perhaps a serious illness has made her forget everything.

It's raining now, and a strong wind blows. Loud thunder sends Okema running to me. I hold him close to me. What is he afraid of? 'The rebels came when there was thunder,' he tells me later. We stand because the veranda is so wet.

One of the children starts singing. '*Min latin do, tedo i dye wor . . .* My mother is cooking at night.' I join in, happily. It's a song that Laker and I used to sing when we were young.

Soon we are all singing. The night is cold and wet, but the song helps us feel warm, and we are safe in town away from the rebels.

❄

In the morning it feels good to be still alive. As Okema and the others run home to get ready for school, I go to Gulu Hospital again. I can't take anything to give Laker. There isn't much food around and I have no more money.

Today, as I sit beside her bed, I hold her hands and repeatedly tell her, 'I'm *Won* Okech's Atita.'

'*Otoo. Won* Okech *otoo,*' she replies.

'Yes. *Won* Okech is dead,' I say.

She reaches out to feel my face. I hope that today she'll

*Laker reaches out to feel my face. I hope that today
she'll remember me.*

remember me. Her hands move over my face and stop at the scar under my chin. Is she remembering? I got that scar when I fell off a seesaw once.

Then she looks at my neck. She used to like the lines round my neck. She always said I didn't need to wear a necklace because I had a natural one. She used to say to me, 'Atita, Atita, bangle-necked Atita.' If she says it now, I will know that she has remembered me.

I watch her face and wait, hoping and hoping for a smile, which will tell me that she knows me. Suddenly she pulls away from me. Her eyes are empty, without expression.

I want to sit here until she remembers me. I've learnt she was found lying in the street near the hospital. No one knows her story, but it will be the usual one. If she can remember the past and the good times, perhaps it will help her get better. She hasn't talked since she came here.

'Laker,' I call.

No answer, nothing.

'I have something to show you,' I say.

I take out the photo and hold it before her eyes. I hold my breath, hoping she will remember. She stares at it.

'Do you remember?'

I point to the faces.

'See, you're here in the photo. I am beside you. Atita. See, there are the others – Oyella, Adongping, Lamwaka.'

I'm getting restless. Perhaps Laker will never remember anything. But I'm sure she can tell me about the others. Five bright smiling faces in a photo . . . Five green bottles standing on a wall . . . Which of us fell first?

I come here every day. I have to help Laker. Each time I say *Won* Okech, she gives the same reply,

'*Otoo. Won* Okech *otoo.*'

'Yes. *Won* Okech *otoo.*' I repeat her words, but I'd like to tell her about my little friend, Okema, who wants to become President and end the war. No more sleeping on verandas to escape the rebels. A life when we can laugh and grow fat from being lazy. Okema wants to make that happen.

◉

Another evening on the veranda. Okema asks about Laker.

'She's fine,' I say without looking at him. 'Nearly fine.'

'You should leave Gulu,' Okema says, 'and go back to your comfortable life, where you lived before. It's crazy looking for friends who won't remember you.'

I spend the nights on the veranda because my friends lived like this while I slept safe and warm. I am ashamed that I was not with them. The rain washes away the pain in my heart. I tell Okema he cannot understand why I visit Laker every day.

A cameraman walks past, and takes pictures of us. Okema spits at him.

'Why did you spit at him?' I ask.

'He's making money out of our misery.'

'Perhaps he's from the newspapers.'

'You're new to this business of homelessness.'

Okema is right. I know nothing about this nightlife.

Tonight we hear heavy gunshots. The voices of the other children stop, and the radio is turned off. Okema recognizes the kind of gun. He knows all the different guns and the sounds they make.

❋

Laker manages a smile today. She's a little friendlier. Again her fingers feel my face and the scar under my chin. She touches it with one finger . . . Perhaps the scar is saying something to her. She smiles.

'Atita?' she whispers.

'Yes, Atita, *Won* Okech's Atita.' I take her hand.

'*Otoo. Won* Okech *otoo.*'

'I'm here,' I whisper.

Laker pulls away her hand and starts rocking on the bed. I look in her eyes and find myself travelling down a dirt road. Now I'm behind *Won* Okech's house. The five of us are standing under a mango tree, laughing. We have just made a seesaw. I sit on one end, then Laker jumps on the other. As the seesaw goes up, I fall off and my chin hits the ground. I scream in pain.

Laker stops rocking. Her eyes are empty again. My heart is beating fast, as I remember what happened that day.

❋

Okema sits on the veranda, studying. His examination is soon. I don't talk to him this evening. I let him read. He has to work on his dream of becoming President. Who knows? He may bring us the peace that he promises.

❋

When I visit Laker next morning, it's like the first day. There is no expression on her face. And I have so many questions to ask her! I help her to sit up and drink some black tea. I pull out the torn photo and point to the other girls.

'Laker, tell me about Oyella?'

She looks at me. Her eyes tell me she recognizes the name. 'What happened to Oyella?' I ask.

She suddenly seems to be in pain. She starts rocking. I try to calm her, but she only rocks faster. Her eyes take on a dreamy look, and her words are hurried and strange.

'The men came to the village and took them away. They tied them with ropes and made them walk a long way. Some of the men hit the girls with sticks or with their guns, to make them go faster. Someone fell, and stayed on the ground. She turned her face. OYELLA. Our Oyella. One of the gunmen shouted to her to get up. On her face was fear, and then, nothing. She was ready to die.

—Do you want to rest? the man asked.

—Yes, she said in a weak voice.

—You can have your wish, he laughed as he shot her between the eyes.

She made no sound. Later, the other girl ran away and came to Gulu Hospital.'

Laker stops rocking. She's breathing fast. She starts laughing wildly, crazily. I leave her bedside and run outside. I cry. In the photo Oyella's smile has gone and so has her face. Instead, there's a patch of grey. I stare at the sky. It's still blue, and the hospital still stands there.

❉

'Oyella is dead,' I tell Okema that evening.

'I'm sorry,' he says and holds my hand. We sit close together on the veranda. It's another cold, starry night. I look up at the sky and see a full moon. Perhaps the gods up there are looking down at us and laughing at our misery.

*Laker likes it here, lying under the large mango tree,
with her head on my knees.*

'One day this will end,' Okema says.

'Yes,' I say hopelessly.

❄

Today Laker smiles brightly when she sees me. She looks different now, with her hair cut and clean. The wild look has gone. As I sit beside her, she touches the scar under my chin.

I help her off the bed. We walk slowly to the door and go outside, where we sit under the large mango tree. She likes it here, and lies on her back with her head on my knees. I don't know how long we sit there under the mango tree. We watch the sun disappear and see the shadows get longer as they fall on the hospital windows. Laker lifts her head and looks at me.

'What's that song we used to sing?' she asks.

I smile. '*Min latin do, tedo i dye wor* . . . My mother is cooking at night,' I sing quietly.

She closes her eyes and listens to me. Then she opens her eyes. I feel her looking fixedly at my scar, then at my neck. She laughs lightly.

'Atita, bangle-necked Atita,' she whispers.

A smile comes to her lips, very slowly, it lights up, and burns brightly like a flame. She remembered!

A Gathering of Bald Men

MANDLA LANGA

A story from South Africa, retold by Clare West

Modern life is full of worries – money problems, your daughter's unsuitable boyfriend, your wife who doesn't understand you, your boss at work who doesn't listen to your good ideas . . .

Caleb Zungu is not a happy man. He sells insurance to people who don't want to pay for it, he worries about the money that he owes the bank – and he discovers he is going bald. A man can only take so much . . .

Caleb Zungu was forty-three years old, married to Nothando for thirteen years, with two girl children – Busi, who was eight, and Khwezi, who was fourteen. He owned a house in Johannesburg, a car, and two dogs. He was a salesman for a large insurance company, Allied Life, where he had worked for five years. He owed money to the bank, and hoped that God would help him, perhaps with the death of a long-lost uncle, who would leave him some money. Nothando had a full-time job at Transtar, a bus company. The girls were on school holidays, as it was April, and the dogs, which no one called by their real names, were happy with life.

On this Monday, Caleb woke up, took a shower, brushed his teeth, and put his clothes on. He looked handsome, and frighteningly well dressed, in his dark blue suit, white shirt, and black shoes. He drank his coffee quickly and went back to the bathroom. Nothando almost dropped her coffee cup when she heard a scream coming from there. 'Perhaps he's ill!' she thought, and ran to see what the matter was.

She found Caleb in front of the mirror, feeling the top of his head with his hand. He had discovered a bald patch, the size of a coin, and he was very miserable about it.

'What babies men are!' thought Nothando. To her husband she said kindly, 'But Caleb, baldness just shows how strong and sexy you are, every woman knows that! You're looking very good today!' He did not reply.

Later she waved to him as usual as he drove away in his bright pink car, an old Renault which he had never found the time to repaint. But she knew that he was still deeply worried, because he hadn't even taken his mobile phone.

While she was getting ready for work, she thought about her daughters. Khwezi spent too much time talking to her friends on the phone and listening to her favourite music. Now she'd even written 'I Love JM' on her trainers. 'Who the hell is JM?' thought Nothando. 'Probably one of those awful boys who wait around on street corners, watching the girls. My daughter is not going to have a boyfriend like that!'

Her helper arrived to take care of the girls, and Nothando left for work in her friend Marcia's car. Now she was thinking about her husband's problem. 'Some men have killed themselves when they've lost their hair,' she thought. 'What

*Nothando found Caleb in front of the mirror, feeling
the top of his head with his hand.*

a terrible thing to do! You've no chance of going to heaven if you kill yourself. Surely Caleb isn't thinking about suicide, is he? I'll be as angry as hell if he tries something like that!'

At that moment, Caleb was in the Allied Life office, where the manager, Arnold Spicer, was accusing all the salesmen of laziness. 'More and more people are growing older,' he told them, waving his arms angrily. 'They worry about death, so they need insurance. And you all sit here doing nothing about it, when you should be out there in the streets, selling!'

Caleb wished he had a full head of hair, like Spicer. 'Easy for him to say that,' he thought. 'He doesn't have to go out looking for customers. It's more difficult for me than the others. I'm the only one who has to sell insurance to black people. Most of them just don't want to pay for it! And the ones who do, well, they make sure they're never at home when I arrive to collect the money every month. It's not surprising I'm losing my hair.' And for the first time in many months, he decided he'd like a drink.

As he drove along Empire Road, he tried to think of famous men who were bald. There was Winston Churchill – some women found him sexy. What about Gandhi? Well, Gandhi was famous for other things. Bruce Willis? Was he really hairless? He was an actor, so perhaps his head was also acting bald. A bald President Mandela would help – then people would realize it wasn't so bad to be bald, and lots of men like Caleb would walk around with their heads held high.

He parked his car on Pretoria Street and went into the bar at the corner. It was early for a drink – only 11.30 in the morning – but Caleb told himself it was an unusual day. Inside the bar there was loud African music, and the low lighting made the place seem mysterious and a little frightening. Dark men in the shadows spoke quietly to each other over their drinks, and women in bright dresses danced with each other. Caleb knew it was a favourite place for criminals. 'Does it have fire insurance?' he wondered.

He chose a table, sat down, and ordered a beer from the waiter. The music filled the room, and beat inside his head. He was on his third beer, when the dancing women were beginning to look sexy, and he started thinking about suicide. He cried into his glass as he thought of Nothando and his daughters. 'What will happen to them? There's the money that I owe, and of course the funeral will cost a lot. Nothando will have nothing, and the children will hate me for ever.'

But it was just as bad to go on living. He knew that losing his hair was the beginning of the end for him. 'If I can't find any more customers, I'll lose my job,' he thought. 'In a few months from now, I could be a beggar on a street corner, holding a notice that says "Wife and children hungry. Please help". My daughters would be so ashamed of me! Yes, death must be better than that.'

Already feeling less miserable, he put some money on the table, and stood up to leave. It was then that a man entered, and came straight over to Caleb's table. He was a very thin white man, completely bald, wearing dirty clothes and an old pair of trainers. He sat down and said calmly to Caleb, 'Take a seat, my friend. You're going nowhere.'

'What do you mean?' asked Caleb. He had no idea why he was doing it, but he obeyed the man and sat down.

'You were thinking of suicide, weren't you?' the man said. 'I followed you here. I told myself, "He's going to do it."' He laughed; it was not a pleasant sound. Then he turned and shouted at the waiter, 'Bring me a beer, double-quick!'

'Forget it, Ranger,' the waiter shouted back. 'I'm not even giving you a glass of water until I see some money first!'

'Who says I need to pay?' the man called Ranger replied. 'My friend here' – and he put a thin hand on Caleb's shoulder – 'is about to kill himself—'

'Now, wait a minute—' Caleb began.

'And it's very stupid to die with money in your pocket, don't you think?' Ranger was enjoying himself. People were laughing; even the dancers stopped for a moment, to look at this fool who wanted to take his money with him when he died. 'What's your name, friend?' Ranger said.

Caleb knew it was time to tell Ranger to get lost. He stood up, then saw the notice that the white man was carrying.

TOM RANGER BLIND SOLDIER
DON'T NEED YOUR PITY BUT MONEY WILL DO
I DRINK AND SMOKE JUST LIKE YOU

'My God!' said Caleb. 'Blind – oh, I'm sorry.'

'Well,' said Ranger carelessly, 'I'm sorry too. Now am I getting my drink, or what?'

Caleb called to the waiter. 'Give the man what he wants, and I'll have another beer.' Turning back to Ranger, he said, 'My name is Caleb Zungu.'

'And what do you do, Caleb Zungu?' asked Ranger. 'You're some kind of salesman, aren't you?'

'Yes, I sell insurance. Does it show?'

'Man,' Ranger said, 'when I came in through that door, I got this strong feeling of sadness, and I knew there was someone here thinking of suicide. When you're blind, you feel these things, man.'

Ranger would try to get money out of him, Caleb knew that, but in an honest way. The streets of Johannesburg were full of beggars, and people with quick and easy ways to make quick and easy money. Caleb never gave them anything, but there was something about Ranger that interested him.

As Caleb and Ranger talked about life and death over their drinks, the bar became more and more crowded. Several men recognized Ranger, and smiled or waved at him. Ranger became louder, until Caleb told him to be quiet.

'A blind man who can see what I'm feeling!' thought Caleb. Something made him think about Allied Life. 'They're blind too. Spicer refuses to accept any of my great ideas for selling more insurance. He just makes my working life impossible. Still, if I kill myself, Spicer and Allied Life won't matter to me any more. I won't miss them, where I'm going!' He was sure there was life after death.

'I don't understand,' Ranger was saying. 'You want to kill yourself just because you're losing your hair?'

'Isn't that enough?' asked Caleb. He didn't want to talk about his problems at work or about the money that he owed.

'I've helped many people kill themselves, and they've usually had stronger reasons than that. There was a man who was jealous of his wife . . .'

Caleb had once suspected Nothando of seeing another

man. Luckily, two of his best friends told him not to be a fool – Nothando was a good woman. He had started following her, hoping to catch her *in flagrante delicto* – caught in the act of having sex with a lover. He knew he was quite drunk by now because he was thinking in Latin, but he drank some more beer anyway. Next time he had an idea to suggest to Spicer, he'd do it in Latin, and see how Spicer liked that!

'So do you want me to help you?' Ranger asked.

'Yes,' Caleb said. 'But don't give me any lessons about the importance of life, or how my wife and kids will go hungry. Don't give me that.' But he needed a plan that would make his death seem like an accident. The eyes of his children stared at him from the bottom of his beer glass.

'How do you wish to die? There are plenty of ways,' Ranger said cheerfully. 'You know, my dad was a hangman. He's unemployed now, which is a pity, but when he was working, he hanged a lot of people. You die of a broken neck when you're hanged – did you know that?'

Feeling a little sick, Caleb shook his head. He stared at his strange friend with renewed respect. Ranger was clearly a bit crazy, but he was also intelligent and had a clever way with words. 'I'd like to talk like him at dinner parties,' thought Caleb. 'If I hadn't killed myself, I mean.'

It was a bright, sunny day when they left the bar. The streets were crowded. Young men stood around in doorways; on every corner women sold fruit, vegetables, watches, cassettes. Children ran about, loud music was playing in shops, the noise of traffic was continuous. The short walk to the car gave Caleb a strange feeling. All these things

The short walk to the car gave Caleb a strange feeling.
All these things happening around him, this was life!

happening around him, this was life! He looked at every single part of it, and tried to remember it for ever.

As they got near the car, Caleb asked, 'What do you do when you're not . . .?' He didn't want to say 'begging'.

'Getting money out of you people with eyes?' Ranger finished for him. 'Playing word games. My plan was to make a word game in many languages. I'm still working on one for African languages.'

Caleb knew how difficult that would be, so he said nothing.

'This your car?' Ranger asked, feeling the shape of the Renault with his hands. 'Give me the keys, Zungu.'

'What?' Caleb didn't think he had heard right.

'I said, give me the keys, I'll drive.' Ranger's voice sounded stronger now, almost violent. Caleb didn't like to refuse, and gave him the keys. Ranger got into the driver's seat, and unlocked the passenger door. Caleb got in, and started pulling at his seat belt.

'No seat belts,' Ranger said. 'You want to die, don't you?' He started the car, and drove away. In a few seconds the pink Renault was going at top speed through the busy streets, and the rest of the traffic had to get out of its way.

'Used to drive in New York,' Ranger said, driving straight through a red traffic light. 'Great city to drive in.' He put his head out of the car window to shout at a taxi driver. 'What's the matter with you, man? You blind or something?'

While all this was happening, it was lunch time at Nothando's office. Nothando was reading *Cosmopolitan* magazine while waiting for her friend Marcia. Most of the young women who worked for Transtar had already left the office. They looked forward all morning to their hour of shopping for clothes; if a manager made them stay at work, they were cross and unhelpful all afternoon.

Marcia suggested going to a restaurant in Raleigh Street, so they got into her car. Nothando was feeling very tired. It was hard having to look after two daughters and go to work. She was also wondering about Caleb. 'Is he going to be a problem?' she thought. 'It's funny, you marry someone who seems to be your dream man, then bang! something suddenly changes him into a fat old man who just makes you cross!'

As Marcia was driving down Raleigh Street, Nothando saw the pink Renault, speeding out of Abel into Harrow Street. She recognized it at once. Marcia said, 'Isn't that . . .'

'Yes! It's Caleb!' Nothando screamed. She heard the loud shouts of other drivers, who had to stop or turn off the road, as the pink Renault drove straight on.

Marcia followed the crazy pink car down Harrow Road, driving at top speed herself. 'Don't worry,' she said. 'I used to be a taxi-driver. I think we can catch him.'

Nothando said nothing, but held on to her seat. 'Caleb, you fool, why are you doing this?' she thought angrily. And the answer came to her: he's trying to kill himself. She suddenly remembered an old friend, Chris, who had tried to kill himself. First he'd attempted to hang himself from the branch of a tree, but it was too close to the ground. Then he decided to lie down on the railway line. He lay there for some time, but that day there were no trains on that part of the line. In the end he went home, hot and tired, but still alive.

There was a loud crash as the pink Renault turned into Rissik Street. Nothando couldn't remember when or how she got out of Marcia's car, but she found herself running towards Caleb's car. It had hit a wall, and was badly damaged. Police cars were arriving and drivers were shouting. Suddenly, Nothando screamed: 'Caaaaaaaaleb!'

This cry rang above the noise of the traffic. Frightened birds left the rooftops and flew into the sky. Policemen put their hands over their ears in pain, car salesmen stopped their sales talk to customers, and the cook in the Chicken Licken restaurant ran out of his kitchen, because he thought the end of the world had come.

A policeman, Warrant Officer van Vuuren, pushed through the crowd to get to the crashed car. He opened the doors, pulled the two men out, and laid them on the road. Nothando ran to Caleb, and cleaned the blood off his face. Calling his name again and again, she looked lovingly at him. She knew then that, although he was a fool and smelt of old beer and dirty socks, she loved him.

When he opened his eyes and smiled, Nothando almost cried with happiness. Seconds later she was filled with anger. She pulled Caleb to his feet, and pushing him against the car, she began to beat him with her hands, screaming wildly, 'Youstupidfoolyoustupidfoolyoustupidfool.' At last, tired of this, she threw her arms around him.

Van Vuuren, who clearly had not read the Police Handbook on Good Policing, was busy hitting Ranger round the face, saying to him, 'How many times have I told you to keep out of trouble? You're giving us white men a bad name!'

'Officer,' Caleb said, escaping from Nothando's arms, 'you can't do that to Ranger. He was only trying to help me.'

Van Vuuren turned and looked at Caleb. 'You stupid fool,' he said. 'You're lucky he didn't kill you. This man has been a problem for us for months!'

'Well, we have to remember, he is blind,' replied Caleb.

'Blind?' Van Vuuren laughed, and turned to Ranger. 'Is that your latest idea? If you try to tell me you're blind, I'll put your eyes out myself.'

'Ah, come on, officer,' Ranger said calmly. 'Don't be unkind. A man has got to live, hasn't he?'

The fun was over, and the watching crowd began to move away. An ambulance came to take the two men to hospital, and Nothando went with them. Caleb still couldn't believe that Ranger was not blind. He wanted to jump up and beat him round the head, but he didn't feel strong enough. It was tiring just thinking about the crazy, crazy things that he and Ranger had done.

A month later, Caleb left his job at Allied Life, and started what he called the Progressive Hairlessness Educational Workshop. His plan was to get people talking about baldness, and to help people accept their hairlessness, not worry about it. PHEW, as it was known, started badly, because reporters found baldness very funny; they said PHEW wasn't a serious business and it wouldn't last a month. But Caleb put a lot of hard work into it. He rang up all his old customers and asked for their help. He found several famous people who were ready to speak about their baldness on the radio.

*Caleb and Ranger travelled all over the country, and everywhere
they went, they took the PHEW logo with them.*

Ranger soon joined him, and together they appeared on television programmes and travelled all over the country. Everywhere they went, they took the PHEW logo – a picture of a large egg with a confident smile and 'Proud to be hairless' written in red below it.

Letters from interested people arrived by every post. There was a heated discussion in the newspapers and on television (by then Caleb had shaved all his hair off and looked completely bald) – could people with thinning hair join PHEW? By now, baldness was discussed openly, and many people sent money to PHEW, to keep the work going. PHEW became a very successful company.

Caleb Zungu was forty-five years old, married to Nothando for fifteen years, with two girl children – Busi, who was ten, and Khwezi, who was sixteen. He owned a house in Johannesburg, two cars, and two dogs. He was the manager of the PHEW Company. Nothando and Ranger also worked for the company. JM was accepted as a future husband for Khwezi, and as a worker in the company, because he had started to lose his hair early.

And the two dogs were called by their real names, Baldy and Beauty.

GLOSSARY

air hostess a woman who looks after the passengers on a plane

alcohol drinks such as beer, wine, and whisky contain alcohol

ancient very old

apart into pieces, not together (the lines *Things fall apart / The centre cannot hold* are from a poem by the Irish poet W. B. Yeats, and *Things Fall Apart* was used as the title for a famous novel by the African writer Chinua Achebe)

apologize to say that you are sorry for something you have done; **apologetic** (*adj*) feeling or looking sorry

attack (*v & n*) to start fighting or hurting someone

bangle a big ring of gold, silver, etc. worn round the arm or neck

beggar a person who lives by asking people for money or food

bewildered surprised and confused; **bewilderment** (*n*)

blind not able to see

blouse a piece of clothing like a shirt, worn by a woman

blush (*v*) to become red in the face

Bwana (*Swahili*) used when speaking to an important man

cheerful looking or sounding happy; making people feel happy

culture the ideas and beliefs of a particular society or country

custom the usual, accepted way of doing something in a society

embarrassed ashamed; worried about what other people think

examination a school or university test

fan (*n*) a thing you hold in your hand and wave, to make cool air

fool (*n*) a person who is silly or acts in a silly way

funeral the ceremony of burying a dead person

gentleman a man of good family who always behaves well

gramophone (*old-fashioned*) a machine for playing musical records

hangman a person whose job is to hang criminals

heaven the place believed to be the home of God; a happy place

hell (what the hell ...?) a word used to express anger or surprise

innocent having little experience of life or of unpleasant things

instinct a natural understanding of something, not based on facts

insurance when you pay money to a company, which promises to pay you if you have an accident, injury, etc.

jacket a short coat with sleeves

landmine a bomb placed on or under the ground, which explodes when people walk over it

Latin the language that was used in ancient Rome

literature writing, such as novels, plays, and poetry

LRA (Lord's Resistance Army) an army of rebels in northern Uganda

mango a tropical fruit with smooth yellow or red skin

nursery rhyme a traditional poem or song for young children

patch (*n*) a small area, which is different from the area around it

pawnshop a shop that lends money in exchange for something left with them (if you want it back, you must repay the money)

pity (*n*) a sympathetic understanding of another person's troubles

professor an important university teacher

proxy (by proxy) when something official is done for you when you are not able to be there to do it yourself

rebel someone who fights against their government because they want things to change

respect (*v*) to admire or have a high opinion of someone

rock (*v*) to move backwards and forwards or from side to side

salesman a man whose job is selling things to people

scar (*n*) a mark left on the skin after an injury has healed

seat belt a belt fixed to a car or plane seat that holds you in the seat while travelling

seesaw (n)   a long piece of wood supported in the middle (a child sits on each end, and makes the see-saw move up and down)

sex   the act of making love

sexy   sexually attractive

sociology   the study of human societies and social behaviour

soil (*n*)   earth; the land that is part of a country

spit (*v*)   to force liquid out of your mouth, often as a sign of anger

stage (*n*)   a raised area in a hall on which musicians perform

suicide   when a person kills him/herself

sweat (*v*)   to lose water from your skin when you are hot or afraid

torn (*adj*)   with holes in; with uneven edges

trainers   shoes that you wear for sport or to relax in

veranda   a platform with an open front and a roof, built on the side of a house on the ground floor

the West   the countries of North America and western Europe

westernized   following ideas and ways of life that are typical of western Europe and North America

Zulu   the language spoken by Zulus and many other black South Africans

ACTIVITIES

Before Reading

Before you read the stories, read the introductions at the beginning, then use these activities to help you think about the stories. How much can you guess or predict?

1 *Ekaterina* (story introduction page 1). What do you think about arranged marriages? Here is a list of points which can help to make an arranged marriage successful. In your opinion, which three points are the most important?

  1 being of the same nationality
  2 living near the bride's family
  3 having plenty of money
  4 sharing the same religion
  5 starting with respect for each other
  6 coming from the same family background

2 *Breaking Loose* (story introduction page 15). Which of these descriptions of a foreigner do you think are true?

A foreigner is a person who . . .
  1 comes from a different country.
  2 does not speak the local language.
  3 can't understand another country's customs.
  4 does not belong in a particular place.
  5 always feels sad because they are away from home.
  6 has lived in a country a long time, but wasn't born there.

3 *Remember Atita* (story introduction page 27). **What can you predict about this story? Guess answers to these questions.**

1 How many of her friends will Atita manage to find, or won't she find any of them?

2 If she finds any of them, will they be ill, or well, or dead?

3 Will it be hard to recognize them? Will she remember them, and will they remember her?

4 Will Atita make any friends among the children who sleep on the veranda?

5 Will she talk to the rebels and ask them for information?

6 What will be the main theme of the story? War? Unhappiness? Love and friendship?

7 Will the story have a sad or happy ending?

4 *A Gathering of Bald Men* (story introduction page 41). **Read this list of things that some people worry about. How serious do you think they are? Put them in order, with number 1 for the most serious, and number 10 for the least serious.**

____ I owe the bank a lot of money.

____ I think I'm going bald.

____ My daughter has an unsuitable boyfriend.

____ My boss doesn't listen to the great ideas I have.

____ My wife (husband) doesn't understand me.

____ I don't enjoy my job any more.

____ I'm going to fail my examinations.

____ I'll have to buy a new car soon.

____ I haven't got any friends.

____ I've put on five kilos recently.

After Reading

1 Here are the thoughts of four characters (one from each story). Who is thinking, in which story, and what has just happened in the story?

1 'Aha, I'm in luck! Look at that man, crying into his beer – he looks really miserable. I'll give him something else to think about – and get a few beers out of him at the same time. I'll get out my little sign . . . and off I go!'

2 'So where is he – the man I'll be with for the rest of my life? There's someone looking at me – coming towards me – oh no! It can't be him! He's so old! And so fat! Aagh, he's horrible! Nothing like his photo! Oh, where's that kind, sweet man from the plane? He'll help me escape!'

3 'Poor girl! She thought everything would be all right when she finally found one of her friends. She doesn't know much about life here. We've all been through such terrible things. You can't expect anyone to recognize you if you've been away. No one wants to remember the past – it's too painful. Ah well, back to my reading and my studies . . .'

4 'I suppose it was a mistake to go. Obviously her mother sees me as a foreigner and I'm not welcome. I just wanted to show a little respect. It's a pity. She's a lovely girl, and I was hoping . . . but I'd better keep away from now on. I don't want to make any more trouble for her . . .'

2 Use these clues to complete the crossword with seven words from one of the stories. (All the words go across.)

1 a feeling of unhappiness (7)
2 an African word for a hot egg sandwich which costs sixty cents (7)
3 an old machine for playing musical records (10)
4 someone who plays the guitar (9)
5 a place where books are kept (7)
6 the ceremony of burying a dead person (7)
7 showing thanks because someone has done something kind for you (8)

1 Which story do these words come from?
2 There is a seven-letter word hidden in the crossword. What is it?
3 Why is this an important word in the story?
   (Clues: What does Daniel say about African writers? What does Yasmin do about her past?)

3 Nothando, in *A Gathering of Bald Men*, probably told her
  friend Marcia, on their way to work, about Caleb's worry that
  he was going bald (see page 42). Complete Nothando's side of
  their conversation.

MARCIA: You're looking unhappy, Nothando. What's up?
NOTHANDO: _____
MARCIA: Why, what's the matter with him?
NOTHANDO: _____
MARCIA: A bald patch? How big was it?
NOTHANDO: _____
MARCIA: Oh dear! So what did he say when he discovered
    this very small bald patch?
NOTHANDO: _____
MARCIA: Just like a man! They think a little thing like that is
    the end of the world. What did you say to him?
NOTHANDO: _____
MARCIA: Well, you're right. Caleb's got nothing to worry
    about. He's looking great these days!
NOTHANDO: _____
MARCIA: Was he? I'm sure he'll get used to it soon. He'll
    forget all about it by lunchtime, I expect.
NOTHANDO: _____
MARCIA: His mobile phone? That's a bad sign.
NOTHANDO: _____
MARCIA: Yes, I've never seen him without it. But he'll
    probably go back for it at lunch-time.
NOTHANDO: _____
MARCIA: That's my girl! Put him right out of your mind!

4 Perhaps Yasmin, at the end of *Breaking Loose* (see page 26), wrote to a magazine problem page and received a letter of advice like this. Choose one suitable word to fill each gap.

Dear Yasmin,
You have _____ a difficult path in _____. You are trying to _____ away from family and _____, and go your own _____. You and Daniel must _____ about this very carefully _____ you decide what to _____. Marriage to him would _____ your mother very much, _____ take things slowly. Don't _____ if some people are _____ to you. What really _____ is you and Daniel, _____ else. Your mother will _____ your relationship one day. _____ only wants what is _____ for you. Show the _____ how much you love _____ other, and everything will _____ fine in the end.
Auntie Leila

5 Perhaps Okema, in *Remember Atita*, tells his mother about Atita. Put their conversation in the right order and write in the speakers' names. Okema's mother speaks first (number 5).

1 _____ 'You children all have to take care of each other.'

2 _____ 'Because her grandfather, Won Okech, died.'

3 _____ 'Oh dear, that won't be easy, will it?'

4 _____ 'All she can think about is finding her friends.'

5 _____ 'What about the new girl, son? What does she do?'

6 _____ 'Oh, I will. And she takes care of me, too.'

7 _____ 'Why did she leave Gulu when she was young?'

8 _____ 'No, she's out every day, looking for them.'

9 _____ 'Ah, I remember Won Okech! Be kind to her, son.

6 **What is your opinion about these ideas from the stories?**

1 'It's so important to be free.'
2 'Soon the idea of having different countries will just disappear.'
3 'You've no chance of going to heaven if you kill yourself.'
4 'People who are locked into their own histories and customs are like prisoners.'
5 'It's always better to die fighting.'

7 **Here is a short poem (a kind of poem called a haiku) about one of the stories. Which of the four stories is it about?**

> Money buys a bride
> for an old, fat, bald husband –
> not a fair bargain.

Here is another haiku, about the same story.

> A warm living thing,
> like a wild bird in a cage,
> wanting her freedom.

A haiku is a Japanese poem, which is always in three lines, and the three lines always have 5, 7, and 5 syllables each, like this:

| Mon | ey | buys | a | bride | = 5 syllables
| for | an | old | fat | bald | hus | band| = 7 syllables
| not | a | fair | bar | gain | = 5 syllables

Now write your own haiku, one for each of the other three stories. Think about what each story is really about. What are the important ideas for you? Remember to keep to three lines of 5, 7, 5 syllables each.

ABOUT THE AUTHORS

JACKEE BUDESTA BATANDA

Jackee Budesta Batanda was born in Uganda, and lives in Kampala. At the age of fourteen she decided to be a writer, and she has been Writer-in-Residence at Lancaster University, England, and Peace Writer at the University of San Diego, California. Her short stories have won several prizes, and she has published *The Blue Marble*, a children's book. She has written a short story collection, *Everyday People*, and is currently at work on a novel. In an online interview in 2006, she said that *Remember Atita*, a story about the suffering of the people of Gulu, was one of the hardest stories she had written. She hopes the Bookworms version of her story 'will be read around the world, and people will know and remember about a people in a country far away from their home that lived bravely.'

JACK COPE

Robert Knox Cope (1913–1991), known as Jack, was born in Natal, South Africa. He became a journalist in Durban and then in London, but in 1940 returned to South Africa to farm, go shark fishing, and write fiction. *The Fair House* (1955), a family history of the Zulu rebellion of 1902, was the first of a series of novels dealing with the white man's influence on black culture and the blacks' struggle to regain their pride and identity. He also wrote several collections of short stories, which are widely admired. Alan Paton, another South African writer, says that Cope's stories give us 'in a few words the scents and sounds and colours of our country'. For twenty years Cope edited *Contrast*, a literary magazine written in English and Afrikaans, and he helped South African poets to make their work better known.

MANDLA LANGA

Mandla Langa (1950–) was born in Durban, South Africa, and studied English and Philosophy at the University of Fort Hare. Growing up under the system of apartheid (which forced black people to live and work separately from whites), he was arrested for his political activities and kept in prison for a time. As a result, he left South Africa and lived in other countries for many years. He worked as an editor, a speech writer, and journalist, as well as continuing his studies and writing stories. He has received several awards for his writing, especially for his three novels, *Tenderness of Blood*, *Rainbow on a Paper Sky*, *The Memory of Stones*, and has also published a collection of short stories, *The Naked Song*. Now that apartheid is over, this KwaZulu-Natal author is back in South Africa. He is a well-known figure in journalism, the media, and the arts, and lives in Johannesburg.

M. G. VASSANJI

M. G. Vassanji (1950–) was born in Nairobi, Kenya, to an Indian family, and brought up in Tanzania. He now lives in Toronto, Canada, and visits Africa and India often. He studied at the Massachusetts Institute of Technology and the University of Pennsylvania in the USA, then moved to Canada in 1978. After the success of his first novel, *The Gunny Sack* (1989), he became a full-time writer, and so far has written six novels, and two collections of short stories, *Uhuru Street* (1990) and *When She Was Queen* (2005). His work has won several prizes, and deals with Indians living in East Africa. He says: 'Once I went to the US, suddenly the Indian connection became very important; the sense of origins, trying to understand the roots of India that we had inside us.'

OXFORD BOOKWORMS LIBRARY

Classics • Crime & Mystery • Factfiles • Fantasy & Horror
Human Interest • Playscripts • Thriller & Adventure
True Stories • World Stories

The OXFORD BOOKWORMS LIBRARY provides enjoyable reading in English, with a wide range of classic and modern fiction, non-fiction, and plays. It includes original and adapted texts in seven carefully graded language stages, which take learners from beginner to advanced level. An overview is given on the next pages.

All Stage 1 titles are available as audio recordings, as well as over eighty other titles from Starter to Stage 6. All Starters and many titles at Stages 1 to 4 are specially recommended for younger learners. Every Bookworm is illustrated, and Starters and Factfiles have full-colour illustrations.

The OXFORD BOOKWORMS LIBRARY also offers extensive support. Each book contains an introduction to the story, notes about the author, a glossary, and activities. Additional resources include tests and worksheets, and answers for these and for the activities in the books. There is advice on running a class library, using audio recordings, and the many ways of using Oxford Bookworms in reading programmes. Resource materials are available on the website <www.oup.com/elt/bookworms>.

The *Oxford Bookworms Collection* is a series for advanced learners. It consists of volumes of short stories by well-known authors, both classic and modern. Texts are not abridged or adapted in any way, but carefully selected to be accessible to the advanced student.

You can find details and a full list of titles in the *Oxford Bookworms Library Catalogue* and *Oxford English Language Teaching Catalogues*, and on the website <www.oup.com/elt/bookworms>.

THE OXFORD BOOKWORMS LIBRARY
GRADING AND SAMPLE EXTRACTS

STARTER • 250 HEADWORDS

present simple – present continuous – imperative –
can/cannot, must – *going to* (future) – simple gerunds …

Her phone is ringing – but where is it?

Sally gets out of bed and looks in her bag. No phone. She looks under the bed. No phone. Then she looks behind the door. There is her phone. Sally picks up her phone and answers it. *Sally's Phone*

STAGE 1 • 400 HEADWORDS

… past simple – coordination with *and, but, or* –
subordination with *before, after, when, because, so* …

I knew him in Persia. He was a famous builder and I worked with him there. For a time I was his friend, but not for long. When he came to Paris, I came after him – I wanted to watch him. He was a very clever, very dangerous man. *The Phantom of the Opera*

STAGE 2 • 700 HEADWORDS

… present perfect – *will* (future) – *(don't) have to, must not, could* –
comparison of adjectives – simple *if* clauses – past continuous –
tag questions – *ask/tell* + infinitive …

While I was writing these words in my diary, I decided what to do. I must try to escape. I shall try to get down the wall outside. The window is high above the ground, but I have to try. I shall take some of the gold with me – if I escape, perhaps it will be helpful later. *Dracula*

STAGE 3 • 1000 HEADWORDS

... should, may – present perfect continuous – *used to* – past perfect
– causative – relative clauses – indirect statements ...

Of course, it was most important that no one should see
Colin, Mary, or Dickon entering the secret garden. So Colin
gave orders to the gardeners that they must all keep away
from that part of the garden in future. ***The Secret Garden***

STAGE 4 • 1400 HEADWORDS

... past perfect continuous – passive (simple forms) –
would conditional clauses – indirect questions –
relatives with *where/when* – gerunds after prepositions/phrases ...

I was glad. Now Hyde could not show his face to the world
again. If he did, every honest man in London would be proud
to report him to the police. ***Dr Jekyll and Mr Hyde***

STAGE 5 • 1800 HEADWORDS

... future continuous – future perfect –
passive (modals, continuous forms) –
would have conditional clauses – modals + perfect infinitive ...

If he had spoken Estella's name, I would have hit him. I was so
angry with him, and so depressed about my future, that I could
not eat the breakfast. Instead I went straight to the old house.
Great Expectations

STAGE 6 • 2500 HEADWORDS

... passive (infinitives, gerunds) – advanced modal meanings –
clauses of concession, condition

When I stepped up to the piano, I was confident. It was as if I
knew that the prodigy side of me really did exist. And when I
started to play, I was so caught up in how lovely I looked that
I didn't worry how I would sound. ***The Joy Luck Club***

MORE WORLD STORIES FROM BOOKWORMS

BOOKWORMS · WORLD STORIES · STAGE 1
The Meaning of Gifts: Stories from Turkey
RETOLD BY JENNIFER BASSETT

BOOKWORMS · WORLD STORIES · STAGE 2
Cries from the Heart: Stories from Around the World
RETOLD BY JENNIFER BASSETT
Stories from Nigeria, New Zealand, Botswana, Jamaica,
Uganda, Malaysia, India, South Africa

BOOKWORMS · WORLD STORIES · STAGE 2
Changing their Skies: Stories from Africa
RETOLD BY JENNIFER BASSETT
Stories from Malawi, South Africa, Tanzania

BOOKWORMS · WORLD STORIES · STAGE 3
The Long White Cloud: Stories from New Zealand
RETOLD BY CHRISTINE LINDOP

BOOKWORMS · WORLD STORIES · STAGE 4
Doors to a Wider Place: Stories from Australia
RETOLD BY CHRISTINE LINDOP

BOOKWORMS · WORLD STORIES · STAGE 4
Land of my Childhood: Stories from South Asia
RETOLD BY CLARE WEST
Stories from Sri Lanka, India, Pakistan

BOOKWORMS · WORLD STORIES · STAGE 5
Treading on Dreams: Stories from Ireland
RETOLD BY CLARE WEST